MR. TURTLE
FLYING
ADVENTURE

ALBERT BIGELOW
PAINE

MR. TURTLE'S FLYING ADVENTURE

MR. TURTLE TELLS ABOUT HIS CHILDHOOD AND EXPLAINS A VERY OLD FABLE

ONCE upon a time, when it was early summer in the Big Deep Woods, the Hollow Tree people and Jack Rabbit went over to spend the day with Mr. Turtle, who lives in a very nice stone house which he built himself on the edge of the Wide Blue Water. Mr. Turtle fishes a good deal, and makes most of his living that way, and knows all the best places, so when his friends came he said that perhaps they would enjoy fishing a little—which they could do and sit in a pleasant place at the same time, and talk, and look out over the Wide Blue Water, which was especially blue at this season.

That just suited the Hollow Tree people, for they enjoyed fishing when they had somebody to pick out a good place, and Mr. 'Possum found a nice stump to lean back against, and presently went to sleep, but was waked up soon after, when a big catfish nearly jerked his pole out of his hands. Mr. 'Possum had to use all his strength to pull it out.

Then he was so proud he didn't think about going to sleep again, and told how all his family had been quite smart at catching fish; and pretty soon Jack Rabbit caught a good-sized perch, and Mr. 'Coon hooked a croppie, which got away the first time, though he caught it the next; and Mr. Crow caught a "punkin-seed," which made the others laugh, because it is a funny little fish; while Mr. Turtle just went right along pulling out one kind after another, without saying a word, because fishing is his business and doesn't excite him.

Then by and by the fish stopped biting, as they 'most always do, by spells, and the Deep Woods people leaned back and looked out over the Wide Blue Water, and away out there saw Mr. Eagle swoop down and pick up something which looked at first like a shoe-string; then they saw it wriggle, and knew it was a small water-snake, which was going to be Mr. Eagle's dinner; and they talked about it and wondered how he could enjoy such food.

Mr. Turtle said that Mr. Eagle enjoyed a good many kinds of food, and that he was reminded of an adventure he once had himself with Mr. Eagle, when he (Mr. Turtle, of course) was quite small. Then they all asked Mr. Turtle to tell them his adventure, because they thought it must have been exciting if it was anything like the snake's adventure which they had just witnessed. Mr. Turtle said it was—quite a good deal like it, in some ways—then he said:

"That was the only time I ever flew, or ever had a chance to, or ever wanted to, that I can remember. Very likely you have already heard how once, a long time ago, I thought I could fly, and persuaded an eagle to take me up in the air to give me a start. That old story has been told a good deal, and I believe has even been put into some of Mr. Man's books for his children to read."

Mr. Turtle paused, and the others all said they did remember something of a story of that sort, but never thought it had really happened, because, knowing Mr. Turtle as they did, they didn't believe any of his family would try such an experiment.

"Well," said Mr. Turtle, "it did really happen, though not in the way you have heard. You are right about thinking my family would not care to experiment in that way, and would not do it unless somebody else arranged it for them and gave the experiment a good start."

Mr. Turtle went on to say that in this case it was Mr. Eagle and one of the ancient ancestors of the little water-snake he had just carried off that had started the experiment, though he thought none of it had been really planned.

"I was very small then," Mr. Turtle went on, "about the size of Mr. Man's fist, though I suppose much heavier, for my shell was very thick for my age, and everybody said that if I lived a thousand years or so I might have a shell as big and thick as the one that Father Storm Turtle, up at the Forks, uses to make the thunder with. Then they would laugh and say that Old Man Moccasin, up at the Drifts, would certainly have trouble with his digestion if he ever caught me; which used to scare my mother, for Old Man Moccasin was the biggest water-snake that anybody ever saw, and there was nobody around the Wide Blue Water that didn't give him room, especially fish-fry, and Mr. Frog, and young turtles like me, and even some older ones. My mother used to warn us children all the time, and scold us every day about going away so far from the house and not keeping a good watch-out for Old Man Moccasin, who would surely get us, she said, unless we were more careful. Then she would tell us to look out for Mr. Eagle, too, who was likely any time to come soaring about, and would pick up any food he saw lying handy.

"Well, it used to scare us when we thought about it. Old Man Moccasin was seven feet long, and I judge about half a foot thick. He could lift himself two feet out of the water when he was swimming, and with his far-sighted glasses on could see a mile. Mr. Eagle was fully twice as big as any of the Eagle family I know of nowadays, and didn't need any glasses to see an article the size of a bug floating on the Wide Blue Water, no matter how high he was flying. We tried to keep a lookout in several directions, but, of course, as we got older without accidents, we grew careless, and our mother used to count us every night and be surprised that we were all there, and give us a good scolding to go to bed on.

"Nothing happened to any of us for a good while, and then it happened to me. I was the biggest and strongest of our lot, and had the thickest shell, and I liked to show how grown-up I was, and would swim out farther, and make believe I wasn't afraid any more of Mr. Eagle and Old Man Moccasin, which wasn't true, of course, for Mr. Eagle could have handled me with one claw and Old Man Moccasin could have swallowed me like a pill and enjoyed the operation.

"Well, one day I was showing off more than usual and had paddled out farther toward the Drifts, saying to the others that I was going to pay a call on Old Man Moccasin. I kept on farther than I intended, for it was a nice summer day and the water felt good. I didn't know how far I had gone until I turned around to look, and then I didn't think about that any more, for a quarter of a mile away, and between me and the shore, was Old Man Moccasin, coming straight in my direction. He was a good two feet out of the water and had on his far-sighted glasses, and I knew he was after me. He was coming, too. He was swimming with a wide, wavy motion, and making a little curl of white foam in front, and leaving a long trail behind.

"I was so scared, at first, that I couldn't do anything. Then I thought I'd better dive, but I knew that Old Man Moccasin could swim faster under the water than on top of it, and see just as well. I began to paddle for dear life toward the other side of the Wide Blue Water, which was a long way off, with Old Man Moccasin gaining fast. I knew he was bound to overtake me before I got across, and I was getting weaker every minute, from being so scared and trying so hard, and I could hear Old Man Moccasin's steady swimming noise coming closer all the time.

4

"Of course it wasn't very long until I gave up. I was too worn out to swim another stroke. Old Man Moccasin was only about twenty feet away, and when I looked back at him over my shoulder I saw that he was smiling because he was so sure he had me. It was an awful smile, and I don't like to remember it often, even now, and that was ever so long ago, as much as three hundred and fourteen or fifteen years, this spring.

"Well, when I saw Old Man Moccasin at that close distance, and smiling in that glad way, and his spectacles shining, because he was so pleased at the prospect, I said to myself, I'm gone now, for certain, unless something happens right off; though, of course, I didn't see how anything could happen, placed as I was. But just as I said those words, something did happen—and about the last thing I would have expected. The first I saw was a big shadow, and the first I heard was a kind of swish in the air, and the first I knew I wasn't in the water any more, but was on the way to the sky with Mr. Eagle, who had one great claw around my hind leg and another hooked over my shell, not seeming to mind my weight at all, and paying no attention to Old Man Moccasin, who was beating his tail on the water and calling Mr. Eagle bad names and threatening him with everything he could think of. I didn't know where I was going, and couldn't see that I was much better off than before, but I did enjoy seeing Old Man Moccasin carry on about losing me, and I called a few things to him that didn't make him feel better. I said Mr. Eagle and I were good friends, and asked him how he liked the trick we had played on him. I even sang out to him:

> "'Old Man Moccasin,
> See you by and by;
> Mr. Eagle's teaching me
> How to learn to fly.'

which was a poem, and about the only one I ever made, but it seemed to just come into my head as we went sailing along. Mr. Eagle, he heard it, too, and said:
"'Look here,' he said, 'what are you talking about? You don't think you could ever learn to fly, I hope?'

"'Why, yes, Mr. Eagle,' I said, 'if I just had somebody like you to give me a few lessons. Of course, nobody could ever fly as well as you can, but I'm sure I could learn to fly some.'

"Then I thanked him for having saved me from Old Man Moccasin, and said how kind he was, and told him how my folks had always told us what a great bird Mr. Eagle was—so strong and grand, and the best flyer in the world—and how we must always admire and respect him and not get in his way, and how I thought if I could only fly a little—perhaps about as much as a hen—I could keep from being caught by Old Man Moccasin, which was the worst thing that could happen, and wouldn't Mr. Eagle please give me a lesson.

"Then Mr. Eagle said, very politely, that he guessed he'd keep me from being caught by Old Man Moccasin, but it wouldn't be by teaching me to fly.

"'You couldn't fly any more than a stone,' he said, 'and a stone can't fly at all.'

"'But a stone can't swim, either, Mr. Eagle,' I said, 'and I can swim fine. I could learn to swim right through the air—I know I could—I can tell by the way I feel,' and I made some big motions with my front legs, and kicked with my free hind leg to show him how I would do it; and I really did feel, the way that air was blowing past, so fresh and strong, that if he would let go of me I could swim in it a little, anyway.

"But Mr. Eagle laughed, and said:

"'You have to have wings to fly with,' he said. 'You couldn't fly a foot. If I should drop you, you'd go down like a shot, and would probably break all to pieces!'

"I was looking down as he spoke, and I noticed that we were passing over Mr. Man's marsh meadows, for we were not flying very high, and I could see locations quite plain, and even some objects. I knew those meadows were soft in places, for I had been there once to a spring overflow picnic. There were also a great number of little hay-piles, which Mr. Man had raked up, getting ready to make his big stacks when the hay was dry. So I said, as quick as I could:

"'Oh, Mr. Eagle, I am certain I could fly this minute. I never felt so much like it in my life. Just give me a big swing, Mr. Eagle, and let me try. If I fall and break, it won't be your fault, and you can take the pieces home to your family. I'll be handier for them that way than any other.'

"When Mr. Eagle heard that, he laughed, and said:

6

"'Well, that's so, anyway. You people always are a tough proposition for my young folks. Much obliged for the suggestion.'

"And just as he said that, Mr. Eagle quit flying straight ahead and started to circle around, as if he were looking for something, and pretty soon I saw down there a flat stone, and Mr. Eagle saw it, too, and stopped still in the air right over it, as near as he could judge, making all the time a big flapping sound with his wings, until he got me aimed to suit him, and I could feel him beginning to loosen up his hold on my hind leg and shell. Then, all of a sudden, he let me go.

"'Now fly!' he says, and down I went.

"Well, Mr. Eagle certainly told the truth about the way he said I'd drop. I made the biggest kind of swimming motions in the direction of one of those little haycocks, but if I made any headway in that direction I couldn't notice it. I didn't have time, anyway. It seemed to me that I struck bottom almost before I started from the top; still, I must have turned myself over, for I landed on my back, exactly in the center of that flat stone, Mr. Eagle being a center shot.

"He was wrong, though, about me breaking to pieces, and so was the story you've heard. Our family don't break very easy, and as I said before, my shell was thick and tough for my age. It was the stone that broke, and probably saved my life, for if I had hit in a soft place in that marsh meadow I'd have gone down out of sight and never been able to dig out.

"As it was, I bounced some, and landed right side up close to one of those little haycocks, and had just about sense and strength enough left to scrabble under it before Mr. Eagle came swooping down after me, for he saw what had happened and didn't lose any time.

"But he was too late, for I was under that haycock, and Mr. Eagle had never had much practice in pitching hay. He just clawed at it on different sides and abused me as hard as he could for deceiving him, as he called it, and occasionally I called back to him, and tried to soothe him, and told him I was sorry not to come out and thank him in person, but I was so shaken up by the fall that I must rest and collect myself. Then, by and by he pretended to be very sweet, and said I had done so well the first time, I ought to take another lesson, and if I'd come out we'd try it again.

7

"But I said I couldn't possibly take another lesson to-day, and for him to come back to-morrow, when I had got over the first one; and then I heard him talking to himself and saying it was growing late and he must be getting home with something to eat for those brats, and pretty soon I heard his big wing sound; but I didn't come out, for I thought he was most likely just trying to fool me, and was sailing around overhead and waiting, which I still think he was, for a while. After a long time, though, I worked over where I could see out a little, and then I found it was night, and, of course, Mr. Eagle had really gone home.

"So then I worked along across the meadows, being pretty sore and especially lame in the left hind leg, where Mr. Eagle had gripped me, though I felt better when I got into the Wide Blue Water and was swimming toward home. It took me all night to get there, and the folks were so worried they couldn't sleep, for some one had seen Old Man Moccasin out in the middle of the water, chasing something, during the afternoon.

"Well, of course I told everything that had happened, and almost everybody in the Wide Blue Water came to hear about it, and they told it to others, and Old Man Moccasin heard so much about how Mr. Eagle had fooled him, and how I had fooled Mr. Eagle, that he moved to another drift, farther down, and probably lives there still. And Mr. Eagle heard so much about the way he tried to teach me to fly that he made up a story of his own and flew in all directions, telling it; and that is the story most people know about to-day and the one that Mr. Man put into his books. But it isn't true, and I can prove it."

Mr. Turtle got up and turned around toward the Hollow Tree people. He had his coat off, and he reached back and pointed to a place about in the center of his shell.

"Feel right there," he said, which Mr. Rabbit did, and said:

"Why, there's quite a lump there. It hardly shows, but you can feel it plainly."

"Yes," said Mr. Turtle, "that's where I struck. It was quite sore for a good while. There was a lump there, at first, as big as an egg. It flattened a good deal afterward, but it never quite went away. Feel how smooth it is. It kept just about as it was when it happened."

Then all those other Deep Woods people came up and felt of the queer lump on Mr. Turtle's back, and said how perfectly that proved everything and how Mr.

Turtle always could prove things, and they noticed the inscription about the old race with Mr. Hare, and said in some ways Mr. Turtle was about the most wonderful person anywhere and they were certainly proud to be his friends.

Then Mr. Turtle said they might all sit there and talk about it a little, while he went in to cook the fish and make a pan of biscuits and a nice salad for dinner.

THE DEEP WOODS
ELOPEMENT

MR. 'POSSUM TELLS ABOUT AUNT MELISSY AND UNCLE SILAS AND THE ROMANCE OF MINTY GLENWOOD

ONE night in the Hollow Tree, when the 'Coon and 'Possum and the Old Black Crow had finished their supper and were sitting around the fire, smoking, Mr. 'Possum said that he thought he had heard Mr. Frog trying off a few notes to-day, over in the Wide Grasslands, so that he knew that it must be coming spring, and Mr. 'Coon said that over Mr. Man's way he had smelled burning leaves, which was a pretty sure sign. Then Mr. Crow said that some of his wild relatives had been cawing about lately, and that was a sign, too. Then they all smoked some more, and looked in the fire, and were glad that winter was about over, and presently Mr. 'Possum said that every time he smelled the spring smell, and heard the spring sounds, it reminded him of something that happened a long time ago, when he was quite young and lived with his Uncle Silas and Aunt Melissy Lovejoy, over beyond the Wide Blue Water. Then the 'Coon and the Old Black Crow begged Mr. 'Possum to tell about it, because they said Mr. 'Possum's stories always sounded so unbelievable, and yet always turned out to be almost founded on fact.

"Well," said Mr. 'Possum, "you remember I told you about Uncle Silas Lovejoy going to the city, once, and coming home all stylish, with a young man to wait on him, and how Aunt Melissy, when she saw them, turned the young man into just a plain hired help and set them both to work in the garden; and you may remember how I once told you about all our folks, including the hired man, being moved by a balloon across the Wide Blue Water and set down right at the very door of a fine hollow tree, which we moved into and enjoyed for a long time—my little cousins and myself growing up there, and some of them still living there to this day."

Mr. 'Possum stopped to fill his pipe again, and the others all said they remembered, and Mr. 'Coon said he always liked the nice slow and reminding way Mr. 'Possum began his stories, as it brought everything up fresh, and one didn't have to be trying to think of what had happened before, but could just sit back and listen. Mr. 'Possum nodded, and lit his pipe, and leaned back and drew a few puffs, as if he enjoyed them so much that he didn't care to go on with his story. But pretty soon he said:

"We lived there till I grew up, and all my little cousins, too, and the hired man stayed with us. He was a very good young man; though, being brought up in town, of course it took him a little while to get used to country ways. But Aunt Melissy was a stirring person and she didn't let it take as long as it might have in another family. Aunt Mclissy was quite primpy herself, and said that she guessed she could carry what style there was in our family (being a Glenwood, and having married beneath her), and that Uncle Silas and the rest of us would do pretty well if we managed to keep up with the work she laid out for us; and that was so.

"She kept Uncle Silas and Winters—that was the name of the hired man— busier than anybody, as she never quite got over the trip to town and the way they came home. She used to set Uncle Silas to peeling potatoes, after supper, for next morning, and would make Winters help my young lady cousin do the dishes, which you would not think he would like; but he did. Aunt Melissy didn't know that he would like it so much, or she would have set him at the potatoes, and Uncle Silas at the dishes.

"I don't suppose any of you can guess why our hired man wanted to help my cousin, Minta Glenwood Lovejoy, with the dishes. I couldn't, even after I saw that he was so fond of the job that he could hardly wait until the supper was cleared away and it was ready for him. I used to wonder how that young man, brought up in town, could take so to such work, and then, after a while, I got to wondering why it took him and Minty Glenwood, as we always called her, so long to get through.

"That was the first thing Aunt Melissy wondered, too. She generally knit a little, after supper, and went to sleep over it, and would wake up suddenly and look at the clock and begin to knit as fast as she could, so we would not think she had been asleep. But one night she slept a long time, and when she looked at the clock it was so late that she said, 'Land's sakes, it's bedtime!' and she went over and shook Uncle Silas, who had gone to sleep with a potato in his hand, and scolded him to bed, and shook up the rest of us, and then noticed that Cousin Minty and Winters were missing, and went straight to the kitchen door and opened it, and found them sitting close together, and Winters holding Cousin Minty's hand and telling her that unless she would set up housekeeping with him he would go back to the city and lead a fearful life; and Cousin Minty Lovejoy looking very scared.

"But she didn't look half as scared as she did when she saw Aunt Melissy, nor the hired man, either. He had to make two trials before he could get up, even after Aunt Melissy told him to, and Cousin Minty Glenwood began to cry, and Aunt Melissy told her to go to bed at once, and made a swing at her, and missed her, as she went by. She didn't miss the hired man, though; and I guess he had something else to think of besides Minty Glenwood and housekeeping, for a few minutes, anyway.

"Then Aunt Melissy Lovejoy told him he could take himself out of that house, and not come back except for meals, and she said he could sleep over in the shop, which was an old, leaky, broken stump of a tree where we kept our garden tools. Then I happened to be sitting in the way, and Aunt Melissy tripped over my feet, and when she righted herself she made a swing at me, too; and if I had not dodged in time I might have been injured for life. As it was, she drove me out with Winters to stay in the shop, and I wasn't sorry, for it was an awful time in our house.

"Next morning, Aunt Melissy Lovejoy was still dangerous, and at breakfast she broke out at things in general, and said the idea that she, a Glenwood, should live to see a hired man sitting up to a child of hers, especially one who was a Glenwood herself, resembling the family as she did, and being named that way, too; which seemed worse, somehow, than anything that ever happened to a Glenwood before, except her own case; and she gave an awful look at Uncle Silas, who got a little spunky—the only time I ever saw him that way—and said he thought that Winters was quite a good fellow and would make as good a husband as he had, meaning himself, of course, and Aunt Melissy said, 'Yes, just about,' and asked him if he wanted his daughter to have as hard a row to hoe as she had, meaning herself, though it was Uncle Silas who had the hard hoeing in that family, if I could judge.

"Well, that night in the shop, Winters and I talked it over, and he decided to go away and take Minty Glenwood with him. He might go to the city, he said, to his folks, who had disowned him because he had been quite wild, but very likely would take him back now that he had reformed and was ready to be tamed by a nice little person like Minty Glenwood. He and Minty would have to elope, of course, and he told me to tell her just what to do, because I could get to see her alone, which he couldn't. There was a little sapling grew near the tree, and one of its limbs stuck out above her window. Winters said he would go out on that limb and bend it down, about midnight, and Minty Glenwood could be there and climb out on it, and they would go away together quite a distance from Aunt Melissy, and live happy ever after.

"So I told Cousin Minty Glenwood about the plan, and just what to do, and she was as scared as a chicken, but said she would do anything to save the hired man from that awful city life he had mentioned. She said she knew something would happen when she tried to climb out her window, but she would have to do it, as it was the only way to get out without going through Aunt Melissy's room, which would be much worse.

"Well, that night Winters and I got everything ready, and had all his things packed in a bundle at the foot of the tree, and a little before midnight by the full moon Winters went up and crawled out on the limb to bend it down, but when he got there it wouldn't bend far enough to reach Minty Glenwood's window—him being a lightweight person, though I've heard he got fatter later on. He couldn't jump on it, for fear of waking up Aunt Melissy, so he came down and said I would have to go out on the limb, and he would stay on the ground with the things, because I was always pretty solid, even in those days. So then I went out and crawled along on that limb, which bent down with me, all right, but didn't quite reach Minty Glenwood's window, and I couldn't see how she was going to get on it unless she jumped, which I never thought she'd do.

"But you never can tell what a young person in love will do. She was there waiting, all dressed in her Sunday things, with a big bundle of what she was going to take along, and when I asked her, in a whisper, if she could jump and grab the limb, she didn't wait to think about it, or to give me notice to get ready, but just jumped, bundle and all, and grabbed the limb with one hand and me with the other, and down we swung, for Minty Glenwood was plump, too, and quite heavy with the bundle, and then she let go and dropped, which I should have done, only I forgot it, and a second later that limb sprang back and sent me sailing up into the sky just about in the direction of the full moon.

"Minty Glenwood landed all right—on her bundle, I heard later—and she and Winters had probably got a good ways on their wedding journey by the time I came down in a brush-heap, where we had been clearing up a new potato-patch. It broke my fall, but it was very stiff, scratchy brush, and when I got out I felt as if I had been in an argument with Mr. Wildcat. I was limping, too, and afraid I was injured internally, for I didn't feel hungry, which is always a bad sign. I was taking on a good deal, and making some noise, I suppose, for when

I got to the shop and was going to drag myself up to bed, I heard Aunt Melissy's voice call out the window:

"'What's the matter with you out there? What have you been doing?' And then all at once she gave a howl, for she was in Minty Glenwood's room, and had suddenly discovered that Cousin Minty wasn't in her bed, and hadn't been in it that night. About five seconds later she came tearing out there in the moonlight and grabbed me and says:

"'What does this mean?' she says. 'Where's your Cousin Minty Glenwood and that hired creature, Winters?'

"I could tell from Aunt Melissy's looks and voice that it was not a good time to tell it just as it was. I said I had done all I could to save Minty Glenwood from sorrow, but I had been bruised and scratched in the attempt, and she could see herself that I was bleeding in as many as fifty places and could hardly walk. Very likely, I said, I would not live long enough to tell all the tale, and that I didn't know which way those two fierce young people had gone, which was true enough.

"Then Uncle Silas came out and pretended to be very mad, too, and said it was a shame the way I had been treated. As for Minty Glenwood, she was not worth hunting for, and he would disown her from that moment, though I knew he was as glad as he could be that it happened, and had a pretty good idea I had something to do with it. Aunt Melissy she stormed and carried on, and said her family was ruined and that she was going back to her folks; but she had got more peaceful-like by morning, and put some poultices and bandages on me, and said she didn't see how in time that little, spindly hired man and a mere girl could get a big, strong fellow like me into such a state, though, she said, of course Minty was a Glenwood and the Glenwoods were always fighters. Then she took me back to the tree, and gave me Minty Glenwood's room; and when she was out Uncle Silas came to sit with me, and I told him all about it, and he laughed more than I ever saw him laugh at anything, especially when I told about how I went sailing into that brush-heap. Uncle Silas always did like anything funny, and he hadn't many chances to show his taste.

"Well, my appetite came back, but I didn't get well till I had to, because as long as I could be in bed and seem dangerous Uncle Silas had an excuse to sit with me, and we had a fine time. But by and by Aunt Melissy made up some of the worst medicine I ever tasted, which she said she thought would cure me if anything would; which it did, the first dose. Aunt Melissy stayed pretty savage, though, until one day word came from Minty Glenwood, who was now Mrs. Winters, that they were living in town, and that Mr. Winters's people were very fine and stylish and well off, and had taken him back because he had married so well and reformed, and she was as happy as could be. Then you ought to have seen Aunt Melissy show off. Any one would have thought she had made the match, and she couldn't talk enough about Minty Glenwood living in the city, and our fine Winters relatives; and told Uncle Silas he ought to be ashamed of the things he'd said about Minty Glenwood, and ordered him to take them all back, which he did. Then, by and by, she went to visit the Winters folks, and stayed a long time, and Uncle Silas and I and my other cousins had the best time we ever had in our lives. When Aunt Melissy came back she looked as fancy and put on almost as many airs as Uncle Silas had the time he came home and brought the young man who by and by was to marry Minty Glenwood."

Mr. 'Possum sleepily knocked the ashes out of his pipe and yawned and looked into the fire.

"Did you or Uncle Silas ever tell Aunt Melissy about helping Minty Glenwood and Winters to get away?" asked Mr. Crow.

"No," said Mr. 'Possum, drowsily; "we knew Aunt Melissy, and thought it was a pretty good plan to let well enough alone."

IN MR. MAN'S CAR

THE HOLLOW TREE PEOPLE HAVE ONE OF THEIR MOST EXCITING ADVENTURES

ONCE upon a time Mr. Dog came over to have supper with the Hollow Tree people, and to tell them some news. This, of course, was after he had become good friends with the 'Coon and 'Possum and the Old Black Crow, and enjoyed dropping in for a smoke and a little conversation, especially about Mr. Man's doings, which always interested the Hollow Tree people and their friends.

So on this particular night, when the supper-things had been cleared away, and they all had lit their pipes and Mr. Dog was sitting outside to enjoy the mild evening, he told them something very astonishing. He said he supposed that they had now over at their house (meaning, of course, at Mr. Man's house) the most wonderful thing in the world. He said it was called an automobile, and was a kind of large carriage, but the strange part about it was that it went without any horse or any kind of live thing at all. When Mr. Man brought it home, Mr. Dog said, their Mr. Horse had been looking over the fence into the road, and when he saw that strange object, with Mr. Man sitting in it, holding to a wheel, go flying by, twice as fast as Mr. Horse could run, also making much more noise, and trailing smoke, Mr. Horse gave one snort and took out for the back lots, and they hadn't seen him since. Mr. Dog owned that he himself had thought it best to go under the house, and that he had spent a good deal of the first day there watching Mr. Man open a number of doors and covers that were attached to the new machine, which seemed to be full of sudden noises that Mr. Man could stop whenever he wanted to, though he was not always able to start them with the handle that he turned for that purpose. Sometimes Mr. Man had to turn the handle until he was quite weak before he could get a single noise, and without the noise the carriage would not start.

Mr. Dog said that at first he had been rather uncertain in his feelings toward the automobile, but that, little by little, he had felt more friendly and had come up closer to look at it, only going back under the house again when it started one of those sudden sounds which seemed to make his head ache. Then he got used to those, too, and about the third day Mr. Man suddenly caught him by the collar and invited him to ride, and put him in the back of the carriage, and tied him there with a strong rope so he wouldn't fall out, and so nobody would steal him, because Mr. Man valued him so highly.

Mr. Dog said that when the automobile started he almost wished he could fall out, at first, or that somebody would steal him, because he was sure it would affect his heart, and that when they got to going faster and faster he forgot about the rope, and even tried to jump out, but the rope was quite a good one, and probably saved his life. Then pretty soon he didn't want to jump out any more, and laid down on the floor to enjoy it, and was sorry to get home. When Mr. Man was ready to start, next time, Mr. Dog jumped in himself, and the faster they went the better he liked it, and now when they went he often sat up in the front seat by the side of Mr. Man, and if the car was all full of Mr. Man's folks he sometimes sat behind on the top when it was folded back for fine weather. Mr. Dog said there was nothing in the world that he loved so much as to ride in an automobile and to go fast. He said they often went so fast that they passed some of the birds, and that then he would bark loudly to show his enjoyment.

Well, when the Hollow Tree people heard about Mr. Man's automobile they at first could hardly say anything at all. Then Mr. 'Possum said he supposed what made it go was some kind of clockwork that Mr. Man wound up when he turned that crank; and Mr. Crow thought he must build a fire in it to make the smoke come out behind. Mr. Dog didn't know, himself, just how the machinery went in, but that Mr. Man called it a motor and had ever so many names for different parts of it, and sometimes said strong words when he took one of the parts out and couldn't get it back again without trouble. The wheels ran on rubber, he said, rubber filled with air, which Mr. Man pumped into them, and when anything happened to let the air out they had to stop, and then Mr. Man would change the rubber wheel and pump a good deal, and say strong words again, especially when it was warm. Mr. Dog said it was a great comfort to sit back in the shade at such times, and watch Mr. Man pump, and hear him say all the things that he used to say to Mr. Dog himself when he had made some little mistake or had come home later than usual. He said he had never prized anything in his life so much as he had that car, which was what Mr. Man generally called it.

Well, the Hollow Tree people were certainly excited. They said they surely must see that new carriage of Mr. Man's, and if Mr. Dog would send them word some day when he was going out they would hide in the bushes by the road and watch him go by. Mr. Dog said he would do that, and that he and Mr. Man generally took an early ride together, before the rest of the family were stirring, to get some things at the store down at Great Corners—mostly, of late, things for the automobile, which seemed to consume a great deal of smelly liquid, and oils, and all kinds of hardware.

Then Mr. 'Coon said he would give anything in the world to see that automobile going by with the smoke streaming out behind, and Mr. Dog sitting up in the front seat. Mr. Crow said he would give anything in the world to see that, and to slip over to Mr. Man's barn some time when nobody was at home, and really examine the new object, and maybe sit in the seats a little. And Mr. 'Possum said he would give a good deal for all that, but that what he really wanted to do was to sit in the car and ride, like Mr. Dog, as fast as the thing could go.

Then Mr. 'Coon and Mr. Crow both together said, "Oh, we never could do that— never in the world!" and Mr. Dog didn't say anything at all—not at first—but sat thinking. Then by and by he said, all at once:

"I know," he said—"I know a way that you can get to take a ride in our new car. There is quite a big space under the back seat where Mr. Man keeps his pump and sometimes other things, but he keeps most of his things in a tool-box on the side, and only looks into the back-seat place when he needs the pump. When we start out for a long trip he puts Mrs. Man's and Miss Man's extra hats and things in there, but there are none of those articles there now. So if you should come over very early to-morrow morning, before Mr. Man is up, and get into that place under the back seat, you would have just about room enough, and while you couldn't see much, except maybe a little of the road through cracks in the bottom, you would be riding all the time, and always afterward could tell how it felt."

Well, that was such a scary thought that at first the Hollow Tree people couldn't do anything but just sit and shiver and think about how grand and exciting it would be, but how awful if anything should happen. Suppose Mr. Man should have to use his pump, what would be likely to happen then? No one could tell. Mr. Dog said they would have to jump and step lively then, sure enough.

So then they talked about it and gave up the thought, and went on talking about it and giving it up some more, until Mr. 'Possum said that, so far, the worst had never happened to him yet, and that he would take chances if the rest would; and Mr. 'Coon said it would probably be the end of all of them, but he'd risk it; and Mr. Crow said he wouldn't care to pass his life in the Hollow

Tree alone, and he might as well go with the others. Then Mr. Dog skipped home as fast as he could go, to listen around and see what Mr. Man's plans were for the next morning, so he would know if they were going on their early trip to Great Corners, as usual, or on some excursion. But he didn't hear anything about a picnic before bedtime, and next morning he was up a little before day, and pretty soon the Hollow Tree people came slipping over, nearly scared to death, and Mr. Dog let them in by his special door to the barn, and they all looked at the automobile, and Mr. 'Possum tried to turn the crank a little, and Mr. 'Coon sat up in the front seat and took hold of the steering-wheel and pretended to be driving, and Mr. Crow said he didn't see how a thing that seemed so cold and dead as that could suddenly come to life and move.

Then Mr. Dog said he heard Mr. Man coming down his back stairs, and they all made a dive for the rear seat, and Mr. Dog put the cushion in place and was outside waiting and barking "Good morning" to Mr. Man when he opened the big barn doors.

Then the Hollow Tree people were nearly dead with scare. Mr. 'Possum whispered that he knew that his heart was beating so loud that Mr. Man could hear it and would think his motor was going, and Mr. 'Coon said if Mr. Man should ever move that back cushion he knew he should die. Mr. Crow said he felt sure this was just some awful nightmare, and that he would wake up pretty soon, and he said of all the dreams he ever had, this was the worst.

But just then Mr. Man got hold of the crank in front of the car and gave it a turn, and then gave it another turn, and then said something, and gave it another turn, and suddenly the Hollow Tree people heard a great number of loud explosions which made them perfectly cold, and then there was just a heavy roar and rumble, and they heard Mr. Man say to Mr. Dog, "Come, get in!" and they felt the automobile begin to move.

That was an awful sensation at first. They could feel that they were going, but the soft rubber wheels did not rattle on the road, and about the only sound was the motor, which they could tell was getting faster and faster as they got out into the smooth road across the Wide Grass Lands, and now and then Mr. Dog barking to them in Hollow Tree language that everything was all right and to rest easy and enjoy themselves—that they were just then passing the Four Oaks, and that presently they would be in the Sugar Hollow Road, and that he wished they could see out and notice how things went spinning by. Then they heard Mr. Man tell Mr. Dog not to make so much noise, and after that things were quieter, and they just heard the steady buzz of the engine, until by and by Mr. Dog barked out that they were at Great Corners and were stopping in front of the store.

The Hollow Tree people whispered to one another that they had certainly enjoyed it, but what a terrible thing it would be if something should happen now, so far away from home, and among so many confusing things. It seemed an age before Mr. Man came back to the car and got ready to start again, and when he did they heard him talking to some other Mr. Man, who asked if he should put the things under the back seat. Then the Hollow Tree people nearly died, until they heard Mr. Man say, "No, never mind, I'm in too much of a hurry to get home; just drop them in behind there, any place," which made them feel a little better, and pretty soon Mr. Man started the motor again, and they felt the car moving faster and faster, the same as before.

The Hollow Tree people couldn't see a thing, but they knew they were riding faster than ever, for they bounced about a good deal, and held on to one another and would have laughed at the fun if they hadn't been too scared. They were pretty anxious for Mr. Man to get the car back into the barn, so they could scamper home as soon as he went in to breakfast, for they had had about all the excitement they wanted. But they got some more in a minute, for all of a sudden, just as Mr. Dog barked to them that they were in the edge of the Big Deep Woods and would be home soon, there came a good deal rougher bumping, and then the car ran slow, and stopped, and they heard Mr. Man say, "A puncture, by gracious! Now I've got to put in a half-hour at that pump!"

Those were awful words. He would be back there in a minute, and then what? For a second or two everything was silent, except that they heard Mr. Man getting out of the car, and they got ready to make a wild jump the moment he lifted the seat cover. But then—right at the instant when they expected him to do it—they heard Mr. Dog break right out into a great, big bark, shouting as loud as he could:

"Come! Come! Come! Mr. Man—it's up a tree!—it's up a tree!—it's up a tree!" and they knew by the sound that he had jumped out and was calling to Mr. Man to come into the woods near the road, and then, a second later, they heard him call to them, in Hollow Tree words—"Now! now! jump and run! Jump and run! Now! Now! Now! Now!"

And the Hollow Tree people didn't have to be told again. All together, they gave a great big push at the cover of the back seat, and lifted it, cushion and all, and scrambled out, and over the side of the car and out the back, and were diving into the deep woods on the other side of the road from Mr. Man, who was looking up a tree and scolding Mr. Dog because he couldn't see anything up there to bark at.

The Hollow Tree people didn't wait to see how it came out, but took out for home, lickety-split, and didn't stop until they were safe in the Hollow Tree. That night Mr. Dog came over to see how they had enjoyed it. He said Mr. Man called him several names because he had not been able to see anything up in the tree, and then had changed the tire and pumped it while Mr. Dog was getting calm. Mr. Man, he said, was surprised to find the back cushion had jumped out of place, but did not suspicion the truth.

Then they all talked it over several times, and were very proud of the great experience, though they decided that they would not try it again.

MR. POSSUM'S CAR

MR. 'POSSUM SHOWS HE CAN INVENT THINGS, ESPECIALLY AN AUTOMOBILE LIKE MR. MAN'S

"YOU may remember," said the Storyteller, one evening, to the Little Lady, "my telling you about Mr. Man's automobile, and how the Hollow Tree people, Mr. 'Coon, Mr. 'Possum, and the Old Black Crow, got a ride in it; how Mr. Dog helped them, you know, and just barely managed to keep them all from being caught by Mr. Man."

"Why, yes," said the Little Lady, "and I do hope they never wanted to take another. They didn't, did they?"

"Not in Mr. Man's car—no, they had had enough of that, but they were very much excited over it, and thought if they could just sit up in the seat and ride, like Mr. Dog, and see things go by, and not be down under it, in the dark and danger, they would enjoy it more than anything. Mr. 'Possum thought about it, and talked about it, more than anybody, and after breakfast, while Mr. 'Coon and Mr. Crow were doing up the morning's work, he used to walk up and down in the sun and smoke, thinking and thinking, for Mr. 'Possum is quite thoughtful and a good hand to plan, when work doesn't strain his mind.

Well, one morning, when Mr. Crow and Mr. 'Coon were all through, and came out and sat on a log to smoke in the sun and admire Mr. 'Possum, and think how smart he was and how well he looked for his age, he stopped all at once, right in front of them, and said:

"I've got it!" he said. "I can do it! I can make one as easy as anything!"

"Make what?" said the 'Coon and the Old Black Crow, both together, quite excited.

"I can make an automobile," said Mr. 'Possum. "I have planned it all out. I am going to commence now."

Then Mr. 'Coon and Mr. Crow took their pipes out of their mouths and looked at Mr. 'Possum, but couldn't say a word, they were so astonished.

But Mr. 'Possum just threw his head back a little and blew some smoke, and said that it had been quite hard to plan and had taken all of his best thoughts, but that it seemed easy enough now, and that he might have it done by night.

Then the 'Coon and the Crow did get excited, and said: "Oh yes, Mr. 'Possum, we'll help you. Will you let us help you, Mr. 'Possum?"

And Mr. 'Possum said that of course he would have to do the most, as he would have to show them how, but that they could do all the easy things, and he said they might begin by bringing down the big wood-box out of Mr. Crow's kitchen, and the big wood-saw, and the hammer, and some nails, and any useful tool that they had borrowed from time to time from Mr. Man during his absence.

So then Mr. Coon and Mr. Crow ran up and lugged down Mr. Crow's big wood-box, and got the saw and all the other tools and things they could find, and brought them out to a shady place, for it was a fine spring day and getting quite warm, and Mr. 'Possum showed them a round tree, quite large, that had blown down during the winter, and told them they might saw it in two, first, and then cut off four nice slices, two large and two smaller ones, for the four wheels. Mr. 'Possum sat down on the end of the log and showed them just how to take hold of the saw, one at each end, and pull first one way and then the other, and walked around and sighted across it to see that they were keeping it straight, and got a little cooking-grease and put on it, so it would work faster, and Mr. 'Coon and Mr. Crow worked, and sweat, and tugged, and panted, and said it was wonderful exercise, and by and by really did get the log sawed in two.

Mr. 'Possum said they had done very well for the first cut, which was always the hardest, and that they'd all better rest and smoke a little, as his mind was quite tired with thinking. But in a few minutes he said they might try now to make a wheel, and see if they could do that as well; and Mr. 'Coon and Mr. Crow went at it again, and after a while got a slice of the tree cut off, quite smooth and about an inch thick, and Mr. 'Possum said it would make a very good wheel, but that they would be likely to improve with each slice, and that they must be very careful to hold the saw just as he told them.

So then they rested and cut off another slice, and rested some more, and cut off another slice, until they had four slices, and were nearly ready to drop from being tired and hot, and were saying how fine it was to have that job done, when Mr. 'Possum said that he had just remembered they would need one more slice, for his steering-wheel.

Well, Mr. 'Coon and Mr. Crow thought they would surely die before they got the last slice off, and Mr. 'Possum brought some water and sprinkled a little on their foreheads, and at last that wheel was done, too, and they were all quite exhausted and lay in the shade a while to rest and talk about it. Mr. 'Possum said it might take a little longer than he thought, to finish the automobile, and that it was better not to hurry so, as new thoughts were coming to him all the time. He said that next year they would make another and probably change the style a good deal.

Then when they were rested he showed them some nice straight limbs of the tree that they could saw off for the axles, and when they got those sawed off, which was easier to do, of course, he measured them and showed them how to shave the ends nice and smooth with Mr. Man's drawing-knife, and how to cut out of a strong piece of board some things he called brackets for the back axle to turn in, because the back axle had to turn, and how to bore holes with Mr. Man's auger, in the back wheels, and drive them on tight, and how to bore holes in the front wheels and put them on loose with pegs to hold them on, because the front wheels have to turn, and how to bore a hole in the middle of the front axle and in the bottom of the big wood-box, for the steering-rod, because the wood-box was going to be used for the body, and the steering-rod would turn the front axle and hold it to the body at the same time.

Mr. 'Possum said that he had noticed that on Mr. Man's car the steering-rod did not stand straight up, but slanted a good deal, which seemed to him a mistake; no doubt if Mr. Man could see their car he would have his changed. Then the 'Coon and the Old Black Crow said, "Of course," and that there never was anybody so smart to invent things as Mr. 'Possum, and that it was too bad he couldn't go over and suggest thoughts to Mr. Man.

The Hollow Tree people didn't get their car done that first day, but they got it a good deal more than half done, and could hardly wait to get at it next morning. They hurried out right after breakfast, and Mr. 'Possum had Mr. 'Coon and Mr. Crow sawing, and boring, and shaving with Mr. Man's drawing-knife, making the crank, which was a sort of double windlass that stood up in the car over the back axle, built so two people could turn it; and there would be a strong strap that went down through a hole in the bottom of the car and around the axle to make that turn, too, which would drive the car. Then Mr. 'Possum showed them how to make a seat for the front of the box, so he could sit on it and drive and steer, because that was the hardest thing to do, while Mr. Crow and Mr. 'Coon only had to be the motor and work the windlass. Then they got the strap off of Mr. 'Coon's trunk, because it was a very strong one, and put it on, and tightened it up, and Mr. 'Possum said as far as he could see there was nothing more to be done with his car, now, but to use it. Of course he might think of new things later, to attach to it, but he didn't see how he could improve it at present, and that they'd better take it out to the race-track and try it.

So then Mr. 'Possum got up into the seat to steer, and Mr. 'Coon and Mr. Crow pushed, but it went pretty hard, until they put some grease on the wheels and transmission; after that it went better, but squeaked so loud that you could hear it all through the Big Deep Woods, and Mr. Rabbit came kiting over, and Mr. Robin and Mr. Squirrel came skipping among the trees, and Mr. Turtle came waddling up from the Wide Blue Water, to see what new thing was going on over at the Hollow Tree. And when they saw what the Hollow Tree people had made they could hardly speak for their surprise. And when they found out how Mr. 'Possum had done all the hardest part—the planning it and showing how—they said they had never been so proud in their lives, just to be his friend, and they all helped push it over to the race-track, and when they got there Mr. 'Possum invited Mr. Rabbit to sit in the front seat beside him, because Mr. Rabbit was an author and would want to write something about it; and Mr. Robin and Mr. Squirrel and Mr. Turtle went down the track a piece to see them dash by.

Then Mr. Crow and Mr. 'Coon took hold of the windlass, and Mr. 'Possum told them not to start too suddenly or go too fast at first, as it might injure the transmission, which was quite delicate. So Mr. 'Coon and Mr. Crow put a little strength on the windlass, but it didn't turn. Then they put some more on it, but it didn't turn. Then they put all they had on it and it turned just a little bit, but very slow. Mr. 'Possum said he didn't think it would be dangerous to go a little faster, and Mr. 'Coon and Mr. Crow turned with every bit of strength they had, and worked harder even than they had at sawing up the log, but still Mr. 'Possum said he didn't believe they were going quite as fast as Mr. Man's car had traveled, and Mr. Turtle called to them that perhaps if he and the others pushed until they got it to going well, and the machinery warmed up, it might run better.

Mr. 'Possum didn't much like to have his car pushed, but he said that Mr. Man's car didn't always start well, either, and very likely had to be pushed sometimes. So then Mr. Turtle and Mr. Squirrel got one on each corner, and Mr. Robin went ahead to kick stones out of the road, and Mr. 'Possum said "Ready!" and everybody did his best, and the Deep Woods automobile squeaked and squealed and started down the race-track pretty fast, but not always keeping in the middle of it, because Mr. 'Possum couldn't steer perfectly the first time, and went from one side of the road to the other, and said it was because they didn't push evenly, and he was as proud as could be of his great invention. Then Mr. Squirrel and Mr. Turtle gave it one big push, and let go, and Mr. 'Coon and Mr. Crow ground away at the windlass their level best, and the car went on quite a ways before it stopped. It wouldn't have stopped then if Mr. 'Coon and Mr. Crow hadn't given clean out and let go of the crank and hung over the sides of the car and said it was all so exciting and they were enjoying it so much that they were quite overcome.

Then Mr. Turtle said he had an idea. He said down not far from his house which stood by the Wide Blue Water there was a smooth road with a good deal of a slant in it, and that if the car was over there and got started down that slant it would very likely almost run itself and move a good deal faster. So they all said yes, that was just the thing, and everybody but Mr. 'Possum took hold and pushed, because Mr. 'Possum had to steer; and by and by they got to the slanting road, which was really quite a hill, and Mr. Rabbit got in again by Mr. 'Possum, and Mr. 'Coon and Mr. Crow took hold of the windlass, and sure enough, that time, the car started well enough, and went without any trouble at all. Mr. Turtle and the others had run a good ways down the road to see them pass, and pretty soon they did pass, going faster and faster every minute, and everybody cheered and waved, and Mr. 'Possum called back to Mr. 'Coon and Mr. Crow that they could turn a little slower, so all could enjoy the scenery.

But Mr. 'Coon and Mr. Crow couldn't turn any slower, and when they tried to hold back on the crank it just jerked them right around, and when they let go entirely they went even faster, for that slanting road had turned into a real hill, and they were going down it as speedy as Mr. Man would go down, and perhaps speedier, and Mr. 'Possum wasn't looking at the scenery any more, but was holding as fast as he could to the steering-wheel; trying to keep in the road, and not doing it the best in the world, though nobody was pushing now.

Then all at once Mr. 'Possum saw something that scared him—scared him so he nearly fainted away, for just then they rounded a turn, going lickety-split, and right in front of him Mr. 'Possum saw the Wide Blue Water. They were headed straight for it, and Mr. 'Possum's thoughts became confused. He could only realize two things clearly—one was that he had forgotten all about putting brakes on his car, to stop with, and the other was that he must stop without delay, or they would all disappear in the Wide Blue Water, and that he couldn't swim.

Mr. 'Possum wondered very rapidly what would stop them, and just then he saw a little tree ahead, right at the side of the road, and he thought that would probably do it. He couldn't think of anything but that, and he steered for the tree as straight as he could, which wasn't so very straight, for he hit on the bias.

Still, that was enough to stop the car, but not the people in it. Mr. 'Possum himself flew into a thick blackberry-patch and lost consciousness; Mr. Rabbit sailed clear over the blackberry-patch, and landed in a boggy place, which was soft enough, but quite splashy; Mr. 'Coon went straight up into the little tree they had hit, and grabbed some limbs and hung on, while Mr. Crow just opened his wings, though he hadn't used them for ever so long, and went sailing over to a nice grassy place by the road, and wasn't injured at all.

There wasn't really anything fatally damaged except the automobile. When Mr. 'Possum came to, and Mr. Rabbit cleaned some of the bog off of himself, and Mr. Crow came back, and Mr. 'Coon climbed down, and the others caught up with them, they all looked around to see what they could find of Mr. 'Possum's invention. Some of it was in the bushes and some in the tree, and two of the wheels they couldn't find at all. Mr. 'Coon said his trunk-strap was as good as ever, which was more than Mr. Crow could say for his wood-box. Mr. 'Possum, who limped and seemed suffering, said, when he looked at what they had gathered, that he felt just about as his car looked—a good deal broken up and hardly worth carrying home. Then he said that very likely Mr. Man had had the same experience with his first car, and that next year's model would be different in several ways.

Then Mr. Turtle took Mr. 'Possum on his back, and everybody said it was very fine for the first time, and certainly most exciting, and the Hollow Tree people invited all the others to the Hollow Tree to celebrate Mr. 'Possum's great invention. They stayed quite late, and when Mr. Rabbit started home he said he would certainly write a poem on all the events.

HOW MR. 'POSSUM'S TAIL
BECAME BARE

MR. 'POSSUM RELATES SOME VERY CURIOUS FAMILY HISTORY

ONCE upon a time, when it was a very pleasant afternoon, and the Hollow Tree people were sitting along the edge of the world, hanging their feet over and thinking, Mr. 'Possum went to sleep, and would have nodded himself off into the Deep Nowhere if his strong, smooth tail hadn't been quite firmly hooked around a little bush just behind him. All the others noticed it, and said how lucky it was that a person of Mr. 'Possum's habits had a nice, useful tail like that, which allowed him to sleep in a position that for some was thought dangerous even to be awake in. Then they wondered how it happened that Mr. 'Possum's family had been gifted in that peculiar way, and by and by, when he woke up, and stretched, and moved back in the shade, and leaned against a stump to smoke, they asked him.

Mr. 'Possum said it was a very old story, because it had happened about a hundred and fifty-six great-grandfathers back. He had heard it when he was quite small, he said, and would have to think some, to get it straight. So then he shut his eyes and smoked very slowly, and about the time the Deep Woods people thought he was going to sleep again he began telling.

"My family is a very ancient one," he said—"one of the oldest in the Big Deep Woods, and there used to be only a few, even of us. That was when Mr. Painter, or Panther, as we say now, was King of the Deep Woods, and he was very fond of our family, which helped to make them scarce, and was one reason why they got to slipping out at night for food, when Mr. Painter was asleep.

"We were a pretty poor lot in those days, and whenever Mr. Painter took after one of my ancestors that ancestor would make for a tree and run out on a limb that was too small to bear up Mr. Painter, and just cling there, because Mr. Painter would climb up, too, and shake the limb, and very often he would shake an ancestor down, like a papaw, and the only thing to do then was to make for another tree, or if the next tree was too far, to play dead, because Mr. Painter did not much like anything he hadn't killed himself. That is how we got the playing-dead habit, which others sometimes try and call it 'playing 'possum,' because nobody can do it so well as our family, and I judge some of our family didn't do it perfectly the one and only chance they got to try it, or else Mr. Painter was smarter, or hungrier, at those times.

"Well, my ancestors got so that they could hold to those limbs very firmly with their hands and feet, and Mr. Painter had a hard time to shake them down, though he didn't like to give up, and would go on shaking all day, sometimes, until my folks would get tired out. They used to try to hold and brace themselves with their tails, too, but we had just big, ornamental tails in those days, covered with thick, bushy hair, and of very little use, like Mr. Squirrel's and Mr. 'Coon's."

When Mr. 'Possum made that remark, Mr. 'Coon and Mr. Squirrel sat up quite straight, and were just about to say something, but Mr. Rabbit motioned to them and said "'Sh!" and Mr. 'Possum went right on, without noticing that anything had happened.

"Those tails were no manner of account, but just in the way, and some of my folks thought it would be almost better if they didn't have them at all, but just a funny bunch of cotton, or something, like Mr. Rabbit's."

When Mr. 'Possum said that, Mr. Rabbit sat up quite straight, and was just about to say something, but Mr. 'Coon and Mr. Squirrel motioned to him and said "'Sh!" and Mr. 'Possum didn't notice anything had happened.

"You see," he went right on, "every little while it happened that one of my ancestors would start up the tree not quite soon enough, and Mr. Painter would just manage to get his claws in that bushy ornament, which would settle it for that ancestor, right away. Of course, my family were proud of those big, plumy things, people being generally proud of their most useless property, something they would be better off, and live longer, without. My folks thought those great tails were handsome, especially our young people, who would walk about waving them and practise carrying them in new positions, and about once a week would do up the long, thick fur on them in little knots, tied with tough, twisted grass, which would make the hair curl and look very showy indeed. Even some of my ancestors who happened to get old acted in that foolish way, and when the fur got thin would wear some kind of false stuff, though any one but a blind person could always tell it.

"Well, one day a new and very handsome Mr. 'Possum came into the neighborhood, from some place nobody had ever heard of before, and none of our folks had ever seen anything like him. He was stouter than our breed and lighter colored, and had a very long, bushy tail that curved in a peculiar way and stayed beautifully curled, without ever being put up in grass at all. He said so, and my ancestors watched him, to prove it.

"That young man called himself Somers, and he certainly became popular with the young Miss 'Possums of our section. They went crazy over him, and of course that made all the young Mr. 'Possums jealous of him, though they would have given anything to be like him. They knew they couldn't be that, so they hoped something would happen to him, and used to tell him of nice new and interesting walks to take when they thought Mr. Painter might be in that neighborhood. Then they would follow, and hide around in the bushes and watch, expecting some time to see Mr. Painter get his claws into that curly blond duster before Somers could reach a limb, or shake him down afterward.

"Well, just as they expected, one day when Somers went out for a little promenade alone Mr. Painter happened along, but Somers saw him first, and made for a tree, with Mr. Painter after him, reaching for that fine plume and just missing it, as the handsome stranger went up the tree and out on a limb, with Mr. Painter right behind and making very savage noises. Then he began shaking the limb as hard as he could, and my ancestors, who were watching from quite a safe place, thought Somers would drop pretty soon, for they didn't think he could be trained to holding on—such a fine person as he was.

"So they watched, very hopeful, and sure enough, about the third hard shake Somers dropped—just let go with his hands and feet, and rolled off, almost as if he really didn't care. My ancestors said that was what it looked like, and that was what it was. Somers didn't care at all, for when he let go and dropped, he didn't fall, but just swung off into space, and stayed attached to that limb, hanging head down, by his tail!

"My ancestors had never been so astonished in their lives, nor Mr. Painter, either. He couldn't believe it. He thought at first Somers had got caught, somehow, and gave one more shake, but when Somers swung back and forth, laughing and calling out, 'Much obliged, Mr. Painter—much obliged for the nice swing!' Mr. Painter climbed down and took out for home as hard as he could, without looking behind him, for he thought it was some kind of magic. And pretty soon Somers climbed down, too, and brushed himself off a little, and fixed his tail in a nice position, and walked along, smiling; and my ancestors hurried to him and said they had just arrived in time to witness his great performance, and begged him to show them how he did it, and offered him anything if he would only teach them to handle those useless ornaments of theirs in that grand way.

"So then Somers told them all about it. He said he was the inventor of the idea, and of the medicine that made it work. He said he was very soon going back to his own people, but before he went he would make up some medicine, which would make their hair and tails both curl, and would explain how to take it.

"Well, they were so anxious about it that he began next morning, and sent out different ones for different things—special kinds of roots, and several sorts of very twisty things, such as grape-vine clingers, and honeysuckle, and a great lot of love-vine—that yellow stuff that winds about everything and can choke even a ragweed to death. Then he put it all into a big kettle, and had them pour water on it and put a fire under it, and he boiled it for two days and nights, without letting the fire get down, and after that poured it off into a big gourd to settle, and told them just what size swallow to take of it, and how to practise the new habit when they felt the curling begin. Then he said he must be going, as his family would be worried about him being away so long, and my folks all gathered to see him off, and gave him as many presents as he could carry, and he went away somewhere to the southeast, and they never saw him again.

"Of course, as soon as he was gone, and the medicine was settled nice and clear, our whole family collected to take it. There wasn't a 'possum in the Deep Woods that wasn't there, and they had to get in line, because every one wanted to be first and be sure to get some of that magic juice.

"Well, perhaps they were too anxious, and took bigger swallows than Somers told them to, or it may be the stuff was a little too strong, or Somers got in too much of the love-vine, which has such an awful twist; or it may be he wanted to play a joke on some of our family for being jealous and wanting to get him caught by Mr. Painter—whatever it was, that medicine had an awful power and did even more than he said it would. When every one had taken a good swallow, except the last one in line—he being a middle-aged person named Waters, who had to take what was left, which was only about a spoonful and very disappointing to Mr. Waters—they all felt the curling sensation begin, and commenced the new muscle-practice Somers had mentioned; and just then Mr. Painter, who had probably heard that Somers had gone, came tearing through the timber, and my folks quit practising and broke for trees and limbs, with Mr. Painter after one plump young chap which he didn't quite get, and pretty soon was shaking a limb in the usual way, only harder, being hungrier than common. The plump young person was scared half to death, never having had much practice holding on, anyway, and in about a minute he was obliged to let go with his hands and feet, and just give up everything, shut his eyes, and drop, expecting next minute he would hit the ground and it would be all over.

"But right there that plump young fellow got the best surprise of his life. He had been so scared that he had forgotten all about Mr. Somers's medicine, but the medicine hadn't forgotten about him. During the little minute he had been sitting on that limb his tail had curled itself around it as tight as if it had grown there. Mr. Painter couldn't have shaken him loose in a week. He hung down just like Somers, only not so far, and he didn't swing much, because that strong medicine had taken up all his slack and there was very little room for play. He didn't care for that, of course, not then. He got brave and very cheerful right off, and called out to Mr. Painter, just like Somers:

"'Much obliged, Mr. Painter—much obliged for the nice swing. Swing me again, Mr. Painter.'

"And when the rest of our folks saw that the same thing had happened to all of them they all let go and dropped, and began calling from the different trees: 'Come and swing us, too, Mr. Painter—stay all day and swing the rest of us!'

"And when Mr. Painter heard that, and looked around and saw all my ancestors hanging head down and making fun of him, he thought the whole Deep Woods was full of the strange magic, and he piled down out of that tree and took out for the bushes, and was never seen in the Big Deep Woods again.

"My folks called after him just as far as they could see him, and when they were sure he was gone they thought they would come down and celebrate. But they didn't do it—not just yet. There wasn't one of them that could unwind himself from his limb, except old Mr. Waters, who had got only a teaspoonful of the medicine, which very likely was just about the right amount. Mr. Waters swung quite loose and free from his limb, and got down without much trouble, and it took him all the afternoon to go around from tree to tree and pry the rest of my ancestors loose, and unwind them, because those new-fangled tails would snap together like springs, and it took several days' steady practice and straightening before they were really useful at a moment's notice. By that time another strange thing had happened: The fur on them had curled so tight at first that it was like very close wool; then it kept right on getting tighter and tighter until it seemed to curl itself clear out, and by the end of the week there wasn't one of our family whose tail wasn't as bare as your hand, except old Mr. Waters, who had a handsome curly plume, like Somers's, and became a great curiosity, the only one that we ever had like that in our tribe.

"All the others thought the fur would grow again, but it never did, and when they got used to its absence they decided they were much better off without it, especially since they had learned the Somers habit, which they said worked easier and better in the new, smooth form. They were sorry, at first, that Mr. Somers had not left them the recipe for that medicine, on account of the new little 'Possums that would be coming along. But they didn't need the recipe. That medicine was strong enough, the amount they took, to do our family at least a thousand generations, and maybe more. Somers never came back, and they never heard of him again. Some of my ancestors used to say that he was not a real person at all, but something that could take different shapes and work magic, just as Mr. Painter believed he did. Anyhow, he was a great blessing to our family, as you may have noticed."

Mr. 'Possum moved over to the Edge of the World in the sun, hooked his tail about the same little bush, and went to sleep again. The other Deep Woods people looked at the way he did it, as if it was something new that they had never seen before.

Mr. 'Coon said: "I think I'd like a little, just a little, of that medicine; Mr. 'Possum's gift certainly would come handy at times."

Mr. Squirrel nodded.

Mr. Rabbit looked out over the Deep Nowhere, and said nothing at all.

THE END

Milton Keynes UK
Ingram Content Group UK Ltd.
UKHW041927310823
427823UK00004B/158